Long Jump High

by

Malachy Doyle

To find out more about Malachy Doyle
and his books, please visit

www.malachydoyle.com

First published in 2012 in Great Britain by
Barrington Stoke Ltd
18 Walker Street, Edinburgh, EH3 7LP

www.barringtonstoke.co.uk

ISBN: 978-1-78112-137-5

Printed in China by Leo

Contents

Chapter 1
Flying Jumps

It was Saturday morning. 4 am.

Pete pulled on his dad's old tracksuit over his pyjamas. He laced up his tatty old trainers, the only pair he had. He strapped on his mega head torch, and off he went into the night.

The park was still locked when he arrived. He knew it would be. So he took a run at the big metal gate and leapt right over it.

Pete raced to the duck pond, full speed to the very edge, and jumped. The jump went out and over and all the way across to the other side.

"I can still do it!" he cried, as he landed. "I **can** do it!"

Pete had always been able to do it.

From when he was a tiny tot, all he had to do was run, and jump, and ... FLY!

He'd learned not to do it when other toddlers were around. They gave him funny looks. Like he wasn't normal. Or like he was showing off.

But Pete had just had his 13th birthday. He had decided, there and then, that it was time to stop worrying what other people thought of him.

Yes, Pete had made up his mind that it was time to make the most of his talents. And have some fun, too.

Pete had a plan.

He'd never been much interested in sport. He felt it was best to avoid it, as much as possible. People might think he was weird, with all that flying stuff. If he couldn't avoid it, like in P.E. lessons at school, he made sure he was rubbish at it. That way no one would ask funny questions.

But the Olympics were coming!

They were everywhere you looked – on the TV, on posters, in the newspapers. Everyone was going on about them, especially in school.

And not only were the Olympics in Pete's own country this time, but most of the events were taking place in his very own home town. That's where the athletics were going to be.

So Pete had decided to come out of hiding, for once in his life. He'd decided to use his very special talent to see if he could **win**! Win **gold**!

And Pete didn't want just one gold medal. He wanted **three**!

Pete was planning to win the **Long Jump**.

He was planning to win the **High Jump**.

And to top it all, he was determined to win the **Triple Jump**.

Pete had made this plan after he had looked in his Big Book of World Records.

In the history of the high jump, no one had ever jumped higher than 2.45 metres.

In the whole history of the long jump, no one had ever made it past 8.95 metres.

And not a single person in the history of the entire world had ever triple jumped more than 18.29 metres.

All three records had stood for twenty years or so. How awesome would it be to break the lot of them?

Well, Pete knew the park gate was more than 2.45 metres high, because he'd made a mark on it one night where the top of his head reached. Then he'd climbed up to the mark, and found that the top of the gate was **still** above his head.

So it must be at least 3 metres high – way higher than the world record high jump!

Anyone could tell that the duck pond was more than 8.95 metres across. It was more like 15, at least.

And Pete knew that it'd be no trouble for him to hop, step and jump more than 18.29 metres – as long as he didn't trip over his laces or something. In fact, Pete reckoned he could **hop** more than 18.29 metres, never mind the stepping and the jumping.

So Pete could beat all three records, easy-peasy!

The other thing Pete found out in his Big Book of Records was that the youngest person ever to win an Olympic Gold medal was Marjorie Gestring of the United States.

Marjorie had won the women's 3 metre Springboard Diving in the 1936 games in Berlin. She was only 13 years and 268 days old at the time.

Not bad!

The youngest person ever to win a gold medal in the Winter Olympics was Kim Yoon-Mi of South Korea. She was in the team that won the women's Short Track Speed Skating 3000 metre relay in Norway in 1994. On the day she won, she was 13 years and 85 days old.

Not bad at all!

Pete didn't count the Winter Olympics as real Olympics. He had always thought it was like School Sports Day for Penguins – like, see who can throw a snowball the furthest ...

But he still wouldn't mind beating Kim Yoon-Mi's record.

And guess what?

On the day of the Olympic high jump finals, in June, in his very own home town, Pete would be 13 years and 81 days old.

On the day of the long jump finals he'd be 13 years and 82 days.

And on the day of the triple jump finals Pete would be 13 years and 84 days.

So he'd be one day younger than Kim Yoon-Mi, and 184 days younger than Marjorie Gestring.

He'd be the youngest Olympic Gold Medal winner, winter or summer, in the history of the Universe, ever!

He'd have won not one but **three** Gold Medals!

And he'd have broken not one but **three** World Records – the long jump, the high jump and the triple jump!

Pete would have set World Records that would last for hundreds and hundreds of years.

How was anyone ever going to beat them? No one – not unless someone else came along who could fly. And what were the chances of that?

Or maybe they would change the rules, some time in the future, and allow you to take part with a jet pack strapped to your back?

No chance!

Chapter 2
School Sports Day

"What's all this, Pete?" said one of the boys. "I see you've put your name down for the School Sports Day."

"Yeah," said Pete. "I thought I'd give it a go, for a change."

"But you're rubbish at sports!" the boy laughed.

"Am I?"

"Yeah! Why do you think you're always last to be picked at football?"

"Am I?" said Pete. "Oh. I suppose I am."

Then the day of the School Sports came.

People stared when Pete turned up in an ancient old tracksuit, baggy shorts and tatty trainers. Some pointed at him. Others giggled.

Pete didn't much like being stared at.

"Why, oh why, am I doing this?" he muttered to himself.

But he knew why. He had something to prove to himself – and to the world.

It was the high jump first. Everyone came over to watch. They were all sure Pete would be first to be kicked out. They thought he'd make an even bigger fool of himself than he already had.

But Pete put the crowd out of his mind and focused on the crossbar.

Just the crossbar.

"I'll show them!" he muttered, and took a deep breath.

Pete ran and he jumped, and he **soared**.

Now he wasn't just some weirdo who was rubbish at everything. Now he was free! Free to fly and jump, higher and higher till the ground vanished beneath him.

Pete twisted in mid-air and went head-first, belly-up, clear over the bar. He landed with a thud on the crash-mat. He'd done it! He'd really done it!

And then he heard the strangest sound. It was something he'd heard many times before, but never for himself.

Cheering!

"A perfect Fosbury Flop!" cried Mr Brown, the P.E. teacher, amazed.

"A what, sir?" asked one of the boys.

"A Fosbury Flop! It's when you go over the bar with your back to it and head first, like Pete just did. It's named after Dick Fosbury, who won gold for the United States in the 1968 Olympics."

He went over to help Pete up. "That was brilliant, boy," he said. "Where did you learn to do that?"

Pete held up his hands. "It just seemed the best way to make sure I didn't hit the bar," he said. In fact he'd been studying it on YouTube, but he didn't want to look too keen.

"You can raise the bar, if you'd like, sir," he said. "I think I can jump a bit higher."

The crowd cheered even more when Pete broke the school high jump record, with an amazing leap of 1.6 metres.

They were almost struck dumb when he went on to smash the long jump record, with a jump of 3.9 metres.

And they were totally amazed when he hopped, stepped and jumped his way to a brand new school triple jump record of 7.8 metres.

"Well, you're a dark horse, Pete," said the coach, as he reached out to shake Pete's hand. "Three school records in your first School Sports Day, and you've never even made it to the top of the wall bars before!" Then he frowned, like he almost couldn't believe it. "We'll have to make the sand pit longer," he said. "And we'll have to put you in for the County Finals."

In fact, Pete had found those jumps easy. He knew he could do much more. But he also knew what he had needed to do to win today. He knew what would impress Mr Brown. And that was enough. He didn't want to go any further or any higher. Not yet, anyway.

Because Pete still didn't want to draw too much attention to himself. He still didn't want anyone to ask any funny questions.

That night Pete set his alarm for 4 a.m. again. He put on his dad's tracksuit, his baggy shorts, his tatty old trainers and his mega head torch, and off he went into the night.

When he got to the park he took a running jump and leapt right over the gate. Then he turned round and leapt over and back again.

He ran to the pond and soared over the heads of the dozing ducks.

"Quack!" said one, alarmed at the sight of a human flying past. "Quack, quack!"

Then Pete raced to the football field. When he got to the goal, he took one great hop, and sailed all the way to the penalty spot.

He landed on the same foot, took one giant **step**, and landed in the centre circle.

Then he **sprang** off the other foot, and leapt all the way to the other end.

"I can do it!" Pete yelled, sliding into the goal like a striker who had just scored the winner. "I can really do it!"

Then he turned round and hopped, stepped and jumped back down the pitch. He soared over the quacking ducks, bounced over the gate and ran back to bed.

He did that every night, when there was no one to see him.

He began to train after school with Mr Brown.

And then it was the day of the county finals.

Chapter 3
County Finals

"Come on, son!" Pete's dad roared.

Pete ran, jumped and flew over the bar.

"Wow!" said Mr Brown. "1.9 metres! That's the highest ever jump in county history! You're amazing, Pete! Totally amazing!"

There was time for a short rest, and then Pete was called for the long jump.

He ran and he leapt and he landed in a cloud of sand, way further than everyone else.

"Incredible!" said Mr Brown. "You're the very first pupil in the County history to break the 4 metre mark!"

And then it was the triple jump. Pete took a mighty run-up, then he hopped, skipped, and flew through the air.

"Fantastic!" cried Mr Brown. "8.5 metres! You're a triple county champ, Pete! Three new records!"

The school had a day off to celebrate.

Only Pete had to go to school, because Mr Brown was so excited at having a winner on his hands that he brought him in to train all day.

"You know what I'm going to do, Pete?" Mr Brown said. "I'm going to enter you for the County Finals."

"But that's what I just won," said Pete.

"Oh, no," said the P.E. teacher. "That was the *Schools* County Finals. I'm going to enter you for the real ones – the ones for adults."

So every day, after school, Pete had to stay back for a training session with Mr Brown.

And every day he made sure he did just a tiny bit better than the day before, so Mr Brown wouldn't ask too many questions.

In the end, the day of the County Finals came round. Everyone was there. All the best runners and jumpers in the county had shown up because word had gone round that the winners had a chance of being invited to the Olympic trials the next month.

And isn't it the dream of every sportsman and woman in the world to represent their country in the Olympics?

Pete was a bit nervous. He wanted to do well, but not too well. He put on his baggy shorts and his tatty old trainers, like he always did, and off he and his dad went.

First up was the high jump. The competition began. They raised the bar once, twice – and then there were only two jumpers left.

The third time they raised it, the other guy failed to make it over.

Pete ran and he jumped. It didn't feel like he'd hit the crossbar but he heard it jiggle as he went over. He must have just touched it.

"Don't drop! Don't drop!" he prayed.

And when he hit the mat and looked back up, there it was, still in place. Pete had **won**! With a jump of 1.9 metres!

"Superb!" yelled Mr Brown. "Only thirteen years old and you've got a new county record!"

Soon it was time for the long jump.

Pete started off slow, then picked up speed as he ran. By the time he hit the end of the take-off board, he was going full pelt.

With his final stride, he pressed his foot flat to the board and took off, high into the air.

He whirled his arms and legs like windmills. And then, on his very first attempt, he broke another county record.

"Incredible!" roared Mr Brown. "5.7 metres! How do you do it, Pete?"

"I don't know, sir. I just close my eyes and go for it."

Chapter 4
The REAL County Finals

The last event of the day was the triple jump. Pete was warming up when a voice next to him hissed, "This one's mine, kid. I've been county champion for the past three years and I've no plans to lose my title to some scrawny runt like you."

The owner of the voice scowled at Pete's baggy shorts and tatty old trainers. The trainers were looking a lot more tatty by now, with all the wear and tear they'd had.

But the trainers were Pete's lucky charms, and so he couldn't stop wearing them.

His dad had come home the night before the County finals with a whole set of brand new gear.

"Thanks," Pete had said, with a big smile. But when his dad sat down with the newspaper, Pete had shoved them to the back of a drawer.

Mr Brown came over as the other jumper walked off.

"Who's that?" Pete asked.

"Oh, that's Edgar Winter," said Mr Brown. "He's the meanest man in the history of the triple jump. He'll stop at nothing to win. Just keep out of his way, Pete, and you'll be fine."

Pete had three tries at the jump. He needed them all.

The first time he stepped off the end of the take-off board on his run-up and was ruled out.

The second time his feet had landed just past Edgar Winter's best mark, but then he had toppled backwards. He put his arms down behind him and so they counted the mark his hands made.

And then he had only one jump left.

So this was his last chance to beat his rival, who was standing watching with a big grin on his face.

"12.6 metres!" boasted Edgar. "Beat that, kid!"

Pete ran, took off, and hopped a mighty hop. He stepped a soaring step. And then he jumped, a jump way longer than he'd ever jumped before. Well, apart from in the park, in the dark, over the duck pond.

"12.8 metres!" the judge shouted. "It's a new County record!"

"Foul! He over-stepped the take-off mark!" yelled a voice. It was Edgar Winter. "I saw him!" he shouted. "I did!"

But they went and checked, and there was no sign of a foul.

"Excuse me, young man," a woman with a clipboard said to Pete. "I represent the Olympic Committee. There are still some places left in the national team. Would you like to come up to Manchester next weekend and see if you can qualify?"

"Some of his results today must be good enough for him to qualify for the Olympics already!" said Mr Brown, amazed and astonished at how well Pete had done. "I mean he's incredible, isn't he?"

"His results are impressive, yes," said the woman. "But he's only ... how old are you, Pete?"

"Thirteen," said Pete.

"Way too young!" snapped a voice next to Pete. It was Edgar Winter again. "You can't let children barely out of nappies into the Olympics!" he said. "You'll be the laughing stock of all the other countries! Mine are the next best results – you'll have to take me instead!"

"Go and get my Book of Records," Pete whispered to his dad. "I left it in the car, just in case."

Pete's dad was back in double quick time. Pete leafed through the book until he found what he was looking for.

"There!" he cried. He pointed to pictures of Marjorie Gestring and Kim Yoon-Mi.

"They were only thirteen when they won Olympic gold. Like me!"

"Well," said the woman, with a smile. "You **have** been doing your homework, haven't you, Pete?"

"But they were only GIRLS!" Edgar snorted. "The real Olympics – the proper Olympics – are the MEN's competitions! And they're for full-grown men, not boys." He sneered at Pete as he said this.

"What complete and utter rubbish!" said the woman. "Are you saying women are second class sportspeople? I'll have you know I represented my country in the high jump! And I can't stand people like you, with opinions like that!"

"That's right, you tell him!" said Mr Brown, with a laugh. "And surely Pete's right – surely you should let him in the team?"

"Only if he reaches the correct standard in Manchester next Saturday," said the woman. "He'll need to qualify under strict international Olympic conditions. I'm pretty sure we've never had a thirteen-year-old in the squad before. It's more than my job's worth to let Pete in without making quite sure he's good enough."

"Of course he is!" said Pete's dad and Mr Brown, both at the same time.

"Well, if he's good enough, then I am, too!" said Edgar Winter. "And you'd better take me as well, in case the kid messes up. I mean, everyone knows you can't count on teenagers. He might just decide to have a lie-in that morning instead. You'd look pretty silly then, wouldn't you? Imagine! Inviting some scratty kid in baggy shorts and tatty trainers to the international trials – and he doesn't turn up! Or he does turn up and he's rubbish!"

The woman gave Edgar a look. It was the sort of look that said "It's about time you shut that big mouth of yours."

But it was clear she knew that if Edgar was good enough, she'd have to let him in the team, too.

"All right," she told him. "You can come up to Manchester with Pete. As far as I know, there are a couple of places still left in the triple jump squad. We'll see what happens on the day."

Chapter 5
Olympic Trials

Pete trained with his coach every day of the next week.

Jumping. Sprinting. Weight-training. Hurdles.

At home he ran up and down the stairs, non-stop, until his dad stopped him so he could have some peace and quiet.

He got up at 4 a.m. every morning, to jump gates, duck ponds and football pitches. By the following Saturday he was fit as a fiddle and ready for anything.

They drove up to Manchester early that morning. Mr Brown was in the front seat next to Pete's dad.

Which meant that Pete was stuck in the back with Edgar Winter.

"This is my big chance, kid!" Winter whispered, just loud enough so the adults in the front couldn't hear over the sound of the engine. "Don't blow it for me, or you'll regret it every day of your life!"

Then he reached over and pinched Pete. Hard.

By the time they arrived at the stadium, Pete was black and blue.

"Oh dear," said Edgar Winter, as they changed into their sports gear. "You've been in the wars, mate!"

Pete didn't answer him. He was determined to get his revenge in the one way that mattered. Out on the field.

It turned out that Pete wasn't the only one who was determined to win. He wasn't the only one who was nervous about failing, either.

Because some people were at the opposite end of their sporting life to Pete. For these people – Edgar Winter, for example – this was probably their last ever chance of getting into the Olympics. And so they were desperate to qualify. Totally desperate.

Soon after the high jump competition had started, the judges had already raised the bar to the height of two metres – the height it had to be for anyone to qualify for the Olympics. It was higher than Pete had ever jumped before!

By that time there were only three competitors left.

On his first jump Pete hit the bar with his stomach as he tried to flop over it. It fell.

On his second jump, he rattled the bar as he went over. He looked up and behind him as he landed on the mat in the hope he'd see it fall back into place, but it didn't.

Most people groaned. One person chuckled.

Edgar Winter, of course.

But on his third and last attempt, Pete did a perfect Fosbury Flop. Up and over the bar, fair and square. Not a touch, not a rattle, not a drop.

He was the only one to do it.

"You're in the team!" said the woman. "Well done, Pete!"

And there it was again. The wonderful sound of cheering.

"Wow!" Pete shouted. He hugged his dad and then his coach. "I'm going to the Olympics! I'm really going to the Olympics!'"

In the long jump, Pete over-stepped the board on his first try.

He fell just short of the 8 metre length he needed to qualify on his second.

But on his final attempt he made a perfect take-off, soared through the air, and landed on a patch of sand that hadn't been disturbed all day.

"You've done it again, Pete," said the woman. "You're going to the Olympics twice over! This is incredible! Truly incredible!"

It was time for the triple jump.

Edgar Winter went before Pete. On the run-up, you could see in his face that this was the most important moment in his life. He wasn't going to let anything – or anyone – stop him getting to the Olympic finals.

He ran, he took off and ...

He qualified on his very first go, with an amazing jump of 17.2 metres!

"PB! PB by miles!" he screamed, punching the air.

"Well done, Edgar," said Pete. "But what does PB mean?"

"Personal best, you fool," said Edgar, refusing Pete's handshake. "Call yourself a sportsman, and you don't know that? Well, there's only one place left in the team now, and there's still six competitors to go. You've no chance! It's miles beyond anything you've ever done before!"

The other five all went before Pete. And every one of them failed to qualify.

Pete sprang and he skipped and he soared.

And he landed just behind the mark Edgar Winter had made.

"17.1 metres! You're in!" cried the Olympics woman.

"Yeah, maybe," hissed Edgar, sidling up to him. "But you won't beat me, kid. Not when it really matters – not when we're going for gold!" He dropped his voice to a whisper. "I don't care what you do in the other two events, but don't try and beat me in the triple jump or I'll have your brains for breakfast!"

And, while no one else was looking, he curled his palm into a fist, and pressed it to Pete's chin. Hard.

"And you know what else I'll have?" he said, moving his fist down to Pete's stomach and doing a twisting motion.

"What's that?" Pete gulped.

"Your guts for garters! Yes, I'll have your guts ..." He punched Pete, quick and light at the base of his stomach. "... For garters, kid!"

But Pete knew something Edgar Winter didn't. Or Mr Brown. Or his dad. Or the whole Olympic Committee.

Pete knew something only you know. And I know.

And it was the reason that, come the Olympics, Edgar Winter was not likely to end up a happy man.

Because Pete ...

... could FLY!

Chapter 6
High Jump

It was the night before the Olympic high jump finals.

Pete had been allowed to sleep at home, rather than in the Olympic village, because he was so young. And because he lived nearby.

So he got up at four in the morning, as normal.

He pulled his dad's old tracksuit and his tatty old trainers on over his pyjamas, and off he went, into the night. As normal.

He jumped the park gates, leapt across the duck pond, triple-jumped the full length of the football pitch and headed back to bed. As normal.

But it wasn't going to be a normal sort of a day, not by a long shot. It was going to be the best day of Pete's life! Or that's what he was hoping, anyway.

The only thing was, when he went back to sleep, all he could see was the ugly face of Edgar Winter.

"I know your little secret, punk!" Winter was saying. "And you'd better not beat me, or the whole world will know!"

Did he know Pete's secret? Did Edgar really know?

When Pete got to the stadium, the jump coach had bad news for him. Very bad news.

"You've got to wear the team strip from now on, Pete. They let you get away with it for the qualifying rounds, but you just can't go wearing that tatty old gear of yours any more. We'd be the laughing stock of the Olympics!"

"But I NEED to wear it, boss!" Pete yelled. "They're my lucky shorts! My lucky trainers!"

He was scared, see. Scared the flying jumps wouldn't work without them.

"I'm sorry, Pete," said the coach. "But you're jumping for your country now, not just for yourself. We're a team and we have to look like a team. You'd be letting the side down if you go out in front of the world's TV cameras looking like that."

"You'd rather I lost?" Pete asked him.

"Like I told you, I'm very sorry," the coach repeated. "But that's the way it's got to be, Pete. You wear the strip or you're not in the team."

And guess who was grinning away in the background, listening to every word?

Edgar Winter.

"I'll do you a deal, boss," said Pete. "I'll wear the strip, all of it, as long as you let me hang on to my trainers."

"But they're falling apart!" said the coach. "They've got no tread left. You'd do so much better in a new pair."

"That's where you're wrong," said Pete. "Totally wrong."

And so Pete still had the tatty old trainers on as he headed over to the high jump finals.

Forty jumpers from all round the world had got to the Olympics. Pete had got through the qualifying rounds, so now they were down to the final twelve.

The bar was set at 2.2 metres.

Nine men jumped, and only four of them made it through to the final round, when all the men still in would have three last jumps.

Pete and two others chose to sit out the first jump, and wait till the bar went higher.

The bar was raised to 2.3 metres.

There were seven men left now. They all went for it this time, but only five got over.

Pete was one of them.

Then they raised it to 2.4 metres – higher than any of them had ever jumped before.

But you know how it is – when you're going for gold, you make a superhuman effort.

Four of the men managed to clear it. The crowd went wild.

So they raised the bar to 2.45 metres, and the stadium fell silent. If anyone got over that, they'd have tied with Javier Sotomayor's world record! And that had been set way back in 1993!

Pete fouled on his first go. He did it on purpose. He didn't want to make it look too easy.

He knocked the bar off on his second go, too. But this time it wasn't on purpose. This time he was just being careless. This time he'd made life **very** difficult for himself. Because now he had only one chance left. Only one or he was out!

On his third and final go, he heard the bar rattle as he kicked his legs up and over. Surely he hadn't blown his chance?

He dropped to the mat and shot a glance back up at the bar. It settled into place.

HE'D MADE IT!

The Russian and the Australian had put everything into their final attempt, but they just couldn't clear the bar.

But then, on his very last go, the American made it too!

So the bar was raised to 2.5 metres. If anyone got over, it would be a new world record!

Pete and the American both failed on their first two attempts again.

Then, on his last try, the American ran the full 15 metres at top speed, took off like a gazelle, flipped, flopped, rattled the bar and ... FAILED!

Then it was Pete's turn.

He ignored the TV cameras. He ignored the crowd. He ignored everything but the crossbar.

He had to get over it, but only just, so no one suspected that there was anything odd about him ...

"Don't drop! Don't you drop!" he pleaded, eyes focussed on the bar.

He ran, much slower than the American. Eight strides instead of the thirteen the other man had taken.

Then he sprang, head and shoulders first. He swivelled round in mid-air and slid onto his back as he went over, kicking his legs free and crashing down onto the mats.

Only then did he look back to check the bar was still in place ... IT WAS!

PETE HAD DONE IT!

He'd won OLYMPIC GOLD!

It was a NEW WORLD RECORD!

Chapter 7

Long Jump

The very next day Pete was up for the Long Jump.

The forty-two men in the event at the start had been narrowed down to the final twelve.

They had three more jumps each, and then the top eight had three more.

So this was it! This was where it really counted!

Pete paced the full 40 metres of the runway, turned round and ... off he went!

He picked up speed as he hit the board. His toes were only millimetres from the end as he SPRANG …

He jumped as high as he could. As fast as he could.

In his mind, he was leaping over a load of ducks, lined up across the water. A bridge of feathers, from one bank of the pond to the other.

"Quack quack quack!"

He soared through the air and it felt like he was flying. Really flying!

He landed in a cloud of sand, and the crowd erupted.

He'd jumped 8.4 metres! He was in the lead.

The Jamaican jumped straight after him. Pete knew he was the greatest threat. He'd won gold in the last Olympics. He'd won the qualifiers by a mile. He was the closest anyone had come to the amazing Mike Powell, the American who had set the current world record way back in 1991, with an incredible jump of 8.95 metres.

But Pete was going to show him. Pete was going to show the world!

8.5 metres. The Jamaican had taken the lead!

On his second jump, Pete ran and leapt and …

8.6 metres! He was back in the winning position!

The Jamaican ran and jumped and …

8.7 metres!

None of the others had come anywhere close, so it was down to Pete's final, final jump. If he didn't do it this time, his dream of the triple was over.

There was a drumming sound, as blood rushed to his head. He felt faint, so faint, but then he was running, full-pelt, towards the take-off board.

He ran, he sprang, he soared …

And then he had to wait for it to come up on the screen. It seemed to take forever.

NINE METRES! He'd jumped a full NINE METRES, for the first ever time in the history of the whole human world!

Yes, he'd broken Mike Powell's record! The record that had stood for over twenty years!

The crowd went mad! Totally mad!

They were cheering, yelling and Mexican waving, all round the stadium.

The Jamaican looked worn out. He'd still got one more jump, but he knew he was beaten – you could see it in his face. He just knew he couldn't go higher. He knew he'd lost the chance of two gold medals in a row.

He ran off the end of the board, stumbled into the sand, and the flag went up.

Foul!

And Pete was the WINNER!

He'd won TWO OLYMPIC GOLDS!

The crowd went crazy!

Pete's dad came running over to hug him.

"You're amazing, son! Totally amazing!"

"Two for the Teen!" scribbled the headline writers from the newspapers.

"Pete the Teen's the Best we've Ever Seen!"

Chapter 8
Bad News

It was the rest day before the triple jump final. Pete was through the qualifiers and going for his third gold.

His tatty trainers, and the fact that he was only thirteen, were worldwide news.

But, as he arrived at the team HQ, he was called over by the coach. Again.

"We need to talk, Pete," the coach said. He led him into the office. "We've got a problem."

Pete's heart stopped. They'd found out about his flying jumps! Someone must have followed him to the park in the middle of the night! They must have seen him!

"What is it now, boss?" he asked. His voice wobbled.

"There's a rumour going round about your trainers," the coach said.

"What sort of rumour?"

"You know, that there might be something special about them."

"Special? What sort of 'special'?"

"Well, you know ... The soles are too thick or they've got some sort of springy stuff in them that gives you a bit of help when you jump. Something that might break the rules. Here, let me have a look."

Pete handed the trainers to him.

The coach held them as far away from his nose as possible. "They're disgusting, Pete!"

"Maybe," said Pete, offended, "but they're mine – and they bring me good luck."

"The soles aren't allowed to be thicker than 13 millimetres," said the coach, turning them over. "And the heels can't be more than 19 for the high jump."

He finished prodding the shoes and handed them back to Pete with a frown. "These are so worn down I don't see how you get any spring out of them at all!" he said. "Look, Pete, I'll be honest with you here. People can't understand how you could come out of nowhere, at your age, and shatter world records. Unless ..."

"Unless what?"

"Well, unless you're on drugs or something ..."

"You know I'm not on drugs, boss!" cried Pete. "I've been tested non-stop for the past two weeks. I've had to pee into some bottle or another every five minutes!"

"Well ..." said the coach. "It's got to be something to do with these tatty old trainers then. That's what people are saying. I mean, why would you be so attached to them when they're pretty much falling apart? Unless ..."

"Unless what?"

"Well, unless you're cheating, somehow. That's what they're saying ..."

"Who's saying all this?" demanded Pete. "And how come they're only asking now, when I've already won the long jump and the high jump? What's so special about the triple jump?"

"Well, to tell you the truth ..." The coach looked embarrassed. "It's coming from the other competitors."

"Other triple jump competitors?" said Pete. He knew what was coming.

The coach nodded.

"Someone in the team?" said Pete. "Someone in my very own team?"

The coach went red.

And Pete knew who it was. The man who would go to any lengths to win. Edgar Winter.

"But, Boss!" Pete cried, "You know what he's like! Everyone knows what he's like!"

"I know he's not the most popular member of the team," said the coach. "But if he's saying it to me now, he'll be saying it to the newspapers if and when you beat him."

Pete nodded. He knew the coach was right.

"We'll have to tackle the problem now, rather than later, Pete," the coach said. "I'm sorry, but I've no choice. We'll have to hand the trainers in to be tested. It's clear to me there's nothing wrong with them, but the last thing we need is the newspapers screaming 'Pete the Cheat!'"

"But that means ..."

"I'm afraid so. You won't have them back in time for the jump-off."

"But that means ..."

"You can't think like that, Pete," the coach told him. "I have every faith in you. It's not the trainers that win for you, it's you. Now out you go and show them what you're made of. Show everyone, especially Edgar 'the Evil' Winter!"

Then the coach found Pete a new pair of trainers. A brand-new, top-of-the-range pair, with as much bounce as the rules allowed.

Pete took the trainers. But he didn't like them. He didn't like them at all.

He ran and he jumped, he did press-ups and warm-ups, but they didn't feel right. Nothing felt right.

He couldn't even try any sort of a flying jump to see if it still worked. Everywhere he went, the eyes of the world were on him. There were TV cameras everywhere.

"**Teen, Thirteen, Dumps his Tatty Trainers!**" a headline screamed the next morning.

"**Pete feels the Heat!**" screeched another.

"**Hero to Zero?**" asked a third.

And "**Can Pete the Feet still win the Triple Jump to be a Triple-Gold Jump-Champ?**" yelled the last one. It wasn't so catchy.

Could he? Would he?

Or would evil Edgar Winter get his revenge at last?

But in a way, Pete was relieved.

Because now he knew that Edgar didn't know his real secret. Edgar thought that Pete's magic was in his trainers ...

He didn't know it was in his feet. Pete's amazing, super-human, rocket-powered feet.

Chapter 9
Triple Jump

"Right," said the coach. "There's fourteen of you left. You each get three jumps. Then the top eight get another three, and the one with the best jump wins. Got that?"

"Got it!" said Edgar.

"Yes, sir!" said Pete.

"Now go out there and give it your best shot, guys," said the coach. "We've had an amazing Olympics so far, especially in the athletics. I'm trusting you two to add the glitter to the gold. Silver and gold, guys! Silver and gold!"

"Gold!" said Edgar. He tapped his own chest and scowled over at Pete.

As Pete followed his rival out of the room, he glanced back inside. The coach winked at him and smiled. He held up his left hand, pointed to his wedding ring, and then pointed at Pete. Pete understood – the ring was made of gold. The coach wanted gold for Pete!

Edgar Winter had different ideas.

"Listen here, punk," he hissed, once he was sure no one was looking. "This one's for me! You do remember that, don't you?" And he pressed his fist to Pete's chin, hard. "What will I have if you don't remember?"

"My brains for breakfast," Pete mumbled.

"And?"

"My guts for garters." Pete felt a churning deep in his stomach.

In a few minutes, they headed out onto the field.

The triple jump isn't always the most popular event in athletics, but by now Pete was world famous. There were cameras and journalists everywhere.

'**Thirteen and Going for The Triple!**' another newspaper headline had screamed, that very morning.

'**No Trainers, no Triple?**' yelled one more.

The last demanded that everyone get behind the country's newest youngest sporting hero. '**For Pete's Sake!**' it screamed.

Out on the field, the other contestants warmed up and stretched. Pete just sat there and watched.

"Up and at 'em!" the coach said, thumping him on the back.

It was time to jump.

Pete broke into a sprint as he headed for the take-off mark.

His legs buckled under him.

"Aaah!" he yelled, falling in a heap.

As the coach ran on to help him up, Pete knew what had happened.

He'd gone back to being a bandy-legged schoolboy. He'd lost his powers!

Pete sweated as he waited on the bench for his second jump.

He didn't want his fear to show, for all the cameras of the world were trained on his face.

This time he managed a hop, and a skip, but they were so rubbish that he realised he wouldn't even reach the sand-pit if he tried to jump.

He had no choice but to run off the track, with his head in his hands.

The red flag went up and the crowd groaned. They'd been sure Pete was going to win.

And then Pete heard the sound of giggling. It was coming from the bench. Guess who?

Should Pete pull out? Fake an injury or something, so no one realised what had been going on?

No! He had to go for it! He'd been working up to this for months. No – for years!

And then it was Pete's third attempt. His last chance. He knew he'd need to clear at least 17 metres to get through to the final jump-off.

Unless something amazing happened, he hadn't a hope. His dream of triple gold was fading into the distance.

"Just relax," said the coach, who had fallen into step beside him on the long walk from the bench to the run-up. "You know you can do it, Pete. Everyone knows you can do it."

Yeah, but that was the problem. Everyone knew he could do it, except Pete.

And once you stop believing in yourself, you're gone. Once you let the fear in, you're gone.

He knew it wasn't the trainers, really.

He knew he'd only been kidding himself that it was his dad's old tracksuit ... His baggy shorts ... His tatty trainers ...

They weren't what made him win. That was just nonsense. That was the sort of thing Edgar thought.

No. What made Pete into a world-beater was the POWER!

The power to run and jump and FLY!

He'd always had it, he'd never lost it, and today – TODAY – he needed it more than ever.

All he need to do was believe – believe in himself – and anything was possible.

All he needed was courage. The courage to look Edgar Winter in the eye and say, "I'm not scared of you! I'm not scared of anyone!"

"You can do it, Pete!" he muttered to himself. He jumped up and down on the spot to get his blood running warm again. To get the magic back into his head, his heart, his legs, his feet. "Come on, Pete!" he said again. "You can do it!"

At last he seemed to be getting used to his new trainers.

He didn't like them. He didn't like them one bit, but now he could feel the blood running through his veins. From his heart, down his legs, to his feet, his toes and back up and round again.

He could feel himself warming up, from the inside out. He could feel his confidence coming back.

He ran down the runway, all springy on the rubber coating as he picked up speed.

One last step and he hit the mark. He forced himself up and out, like he was cycling.

He landed heel-first on the runway and sprang forward on the same leg, even higher than before.

He came down on the opposite foot and leapt forward as hard and as fast and as high as he could. Out he flew, out and over the sand-pit.

He landed feet first and fell forward, not back. He'd done it! A proper jump. A perfect landing. He glanced at the flag-man. No red flag.

He waited for the judge to measure the jump.

He waited for it to come up on the screen.

He knew it was good, but was it good enough?

17.4 metres! He had come in 8th.

"Good job, Pete," he muttered. He'd done enough – just enough – to get into the final jump-off.

The crowd breathed one great sigh of relief.

One person groaned, of course. Edgar Winter. He was already through. But he had hoped he wouldn't have Pete to contend with.

It was a bad day for the Americans – they all dropped out, including the favourite. The Africans all failed to get through to the final jump-off, too.

So all that were left were Edgar, Pete, the Eastern Europeans, and one competitor each from China and Canada.

Edgar was all pumped up and ready to go.

"PB! PB! PB!" he roared, every time he jumped.

It was pretty amazing, the way he got better and better with every attempt. This was Edgar's final fling, and he was throwing everything at it. A good end to a career of being second-rate and a lifetime of bitterness. He'd happily retire from sport altogether if he could win this one. It was his one chance to go out in a blaze of glory.

Pete almost regretted that he was going to have to beat him. But he had to. No doubt about it.

On the first jump of their final three, Edgar soared into the lead with an incredible leap of 17.5 metres.

The crowd roared.

Pete came straight after – the last to jump.

But something happened between him getting up off the bench and arriving at the end of his run-up. The nerves must have come back, all of a sudden. Or maybe it was the churning he got in his stomach when he thought of Edgar Winter using his guts for garters.

Pete totally mistimed it. He stepped off the end of the take-off mark.

The red flag went up, and the crowd groaned.

At least he had two more chances.

On the second jump of the three, the Chinese guy took the lead, but Edgar managed to regain it, with a superb jump of 18 metres.

The crowd went wild.

"I've got to get a proper jump in this time," Pete muttered to himself on his run-up. "I've got to, I've got to, I've got to ..."

But the trouble is, the more you think about something – the more you worry about it – the more chance there is of it going wrong. And that's exactly what happened to Pete.

As he walked to the start of the runway, he felt sick to his stomach. At one point, he thought he was actually going to throw up. Live on TV, beamed all round the world!

In the end he kept his breakfast down, but he could feel his legs give way under him as he ran. He miscounted the number of strides it was going to take – again!

He took off OK, sort of, but he was off-balance. He came down on the wrong foot and fell forward off the track.

The flag went up for a foul.

The crowd moaned. Cameras flashed.

Pete could see the headlines in his mind. **'Teen Tumbles!'**

'Triple-Jump Teen's The Worst We've Ever Seen!'

Chapter 10
Pete the Feet

It was Edgar's final jump. No one had matched his last one, but there was still Pete to go.

Edgar had to make sure of the gold. He ran, he hopped, he bounded and leapt.

And he did it! 18.3 metres.

It was incredible! Amazing! It was a new world record!

He'd beaten the record Jonathan Edwards set for Great Britain in Gothenburg in 1995. Beaten it by one whole centimetre!

Edgar was pumping the air.

The crowd were going completely crazy.

"Old Guy Beats Young Guy!" roared the TV commentators into their mics.

"Pete's only got one chance left," one told the viewers at home. "Can he pull himself together and show us what he's made of?"

"That was awesome!" Pete said to Edgar, as he got up to jump. "Truly epic!"

But Edgar didn't want his praise. "Hah!" he sneered, and elbowed Pete in the guts. "It's not just about the jumping, kid – it's all about the technique. How long have you been doing this – a few months? I've been at it for 22 years! You've no chance against me! No chance at all!"

And off he went, thumping his chest with pride.

But Pete knew that he did have a chance – he could win by miles. Just as long as he got a jump in.

But now he could see there was one thing he hadn't thought about before. One thing he hadn't prepared for properly. The run-up.

Mr Brown had talked about it. The team coach had gone on and on and on about it. But Pete had never really listened.

He'd made it look like he was taking it all in, but really he didn't want to know.

As long as he kept within the rules, Pete just left it all to instinct.

Because the more he had to worry about, the more chance there was of it all going wrong.

See, he'd never had a problem with it before. It had always come easy to him.

You ran, you took off, and you FLEW!

And that was good enough for Pete.

But there was something about it being the Olympic finals …

Something about going for the third gold …

Something about the hopes of the crowd …

The dreams of the nation …

The excitement of the world …

There was even something about the way Pete couldn't pick his nose without being seen on screens all round the globe.

And of course there was something about Edgar Winter and the way he was glaring at Pete from the bench, as Pete prepared for his final run-up.

Edgar's fist was pressed to his own chin and he was mouthing something.

It was "Brains for breakfast." Pete could tell.

And then Edgar's fist dropped to his groin, and twisted.

"Guts for garters," he mouthed, with the most horrid smile Pete was ever likely to see.

But Edgar wasn't the only one to smile. All of a sudden, the fear fell away from Pete's face.

All of a sudden, he could see that Edgar Winter was nothing more than a silly bully.

He might be fifteen years older than Pete, but in his head he was stuck in the school playground.

Pete might only be thirteen, but he was more of a man than Edgar Winter was ever likely to be.

Pete wasn't afraid of Edgar any more. He wasn't afraid of anyone. He wasn't afraid of being different, of people staring at him, whispering about him, envying him ...

He wasn't afraid of the cameras, watching his every move.

Because this was it! This was the moment he was going to prove to himself that he was strong enough to stand on his own two feet. He was going to shout out to the world, loud and proud, "This is me! These are the talents I've been given, and I won't let anyone stop me using them! My name is Pete and I can ... FLY!"

He sprinted down the runway. Just clear of the end of the take-off mark, he did one giant HOP, up and out. It was like leaping over the park gates in his pyjamas.

He landed on the same foot, and did one enormous STEP. It was like he was jumping out over the quacking ducks, in his dad's old tracksuit.

He came down on the opposite foot, and then he SOARED out over the sand. It was like he was flying down the length of the football pitch in the park, in the dark, in his tatty old trainers.

It was beautiful.

Time seemed to stop.

Then he came to his senses. "Slow down, Pete!" he cried to himself, in mid-air.

He knew that it was a foul if you didn't land in the sand-pit. Even if you'd jumped way beyond the end!

"Slow down!" he yelled, for another reason, too. If he went too far, everyone would realise there was something weird about him.

So he made himself drop to the ground, just before he ran out of sand. Made himself land badly, so his hands stretched out behind him. It was better than running the risk of falling forward, out of the pit.

But he was still way ahead of everyone else!

The judge had to jog forward from where he'd expected Pete to land. He was out of breath by the time he got to him.

The judge got out his measuring tape, and it didn't even reach from the end of the board. He had to get another judge, with another tape, to come and help him.

All the while, the crowd was going crazy! Everyone was going crazy!

Well, almost everyone.

Pete waited and waited, watching the screen. He wouldn't believe it till it was up there for everyone to see.

Then up it came.

"18.9 METRES!"

And the stadium erupted.

Pete hadn't just broken the world record – the NEW world record that Edgar Winter had set, only minutes before.

Pete had smashed it to smithereens!

"Incredible!" "Amazing!" "Unbelievable!" roared the crowd.

"Fantastic!" "Superb!" "Astonishing!" yelled the commentators.

Pete had DONE IT!

He'd WON THE TRIPLE JUMP!

He'd GOT TRIPLE GOLD!

He'd broken THREE WORLD RECORDS!

He was the YOUNGEST EVER OLYMPIC CHAMPION, winter or summer, male or female!

There was only one problem.

Edgar Winter.

As Pete looked over at him, Edgar drew his finger across his throat.

Pete glanced up to the screen and there was Edgar, for all the world to see, giving him a death stare!

The crowd gasped.

Then Edgar jumped up from the bench, and ran towards Pete, roaring ...

The coach grabbed him just in time and rugby-tackled him to the ground. The cameras of the world were going from Pete to Edgar. From Edgar to Pete.

Then, as Edgar scrambled to his feet, Pete offered him his hand.

Edgar looked at him.

And looked at him.

And looked at him.

And took his hand. And shook it.

"Only kidding," he said, with gritted teeth. "Well done, kid!"

What else could he say, with a mic shoved in his face? With the cameras of the world on him?

With the team coach on the other side, making it clear he'd be very happy to have Edgar's ... guts for garters!

And so they made their way to the podium together. Edgar and Pete.

Silver and gold.

They'd won silver and gold!

The flags were raised. The national anthem was played.

Pete had a third gold medal hung round his neck.

And guess what his favourite headline in the next morning's newspapers was?

'Pete the Feet's a World-Beater! Sweet!'